Letter from the Translators

Dear Readers,

We frequently bring our talk "The Magical Encounter Between Books and Children" to readers' communities, and wherever we are, we try to introduce children to books. When a child has found a friend in the pages of a book, that child is already on the path to academic success.

Professionally, we come from the fields of applied linguistics and education, areas in which we have published extensively and on which we have lectured in universities around the world. Personally, we are both daughters of the imagination and friends of discovery. As children's authors we have published hundreds of books, and because we are bilingual, we love to share the treasures hidden in the books of English and Spanish speaking authors, which we had an opportunity to do as consultants on the Green Light Readers/Colección Luz Verde series.

It was a pleasure to select these excellent stories with great illustrations for beginning readers and make them available in Spanish in words as engaging as those used in the originals. For the Spanish-speaking child, it will be significant to have access to authentic texts by recognized authors and illustrators in the United States. For the child learning Spanish, it is essential for the language to be not only correct but inspiring.

The early experiences between children and books are key to their future success. Opening the door of wonder, magic, fun, and knowledge through the printed word is the first step for children in loving the world that reading will bring to their lives. With bilingual books, a universal mind can be fostered at very early ages. That is the world our children will need, and we are helping them to get there.

¡Felicidades!

Alma Flor Ada & F. Isabel Campoy

The Big, Big Wall

No puedo bajar

**Reginald Howard
Illustrated by/Ilustrado por
Ariane Dewey y José Aruego**

Green Light Readers   Colección Luz Verde

sandpiper

Houghton Mifflin Harcourt
Boston   New York

Humpty Dumpty sat on a wall.

Humpty Dumpty se subió a un muro.

He did not want to have a big fall.

Pero no podía bajar.

One friend came to the big, big wall.

Un amigo vino a ayudar.

"I will help you. You will not fall."

—Te ayudaré. Ya verás.

"Oh, not you. You look too small."

—Eres muy pequeño. No podrás.

Two friends came to the big, big wall.

Dos amigos vinieron a ayudar.

"We will help you. You will not fall."

—Te ayudaremos. Ya verás.

"Oh, not you. You look too small."

—Eres muy pequeño. No podrás.

Three friends came to the big, big wall.

Tres amigos vinieron a ayudar.

"We will all help you. You will not fall."

—Te ayudaremos. Ya verás.

Humpty Dumpty smiled at his friends.

Humpty Dumpty les sonrió a sus amigos.

"Now I can come back down again."

—Ahora sí puedo bajar.

Walk With Me

Humpty Dumpty's friends worked together to help him get down from the wall. Work together with a friend in this game.

1 Stand beside your friend.

2 Tie one of your legs to one of your friend's legs.

3 Try walking or hopping.

What happens?
What did you learn about working together?

Camina conmigo

Los amigos de Humpty Dumpty colaboraron para ayudarlo a bajar del muro. Colabora con un amigo en este juego.

1 Párate junto a tu amigo.

2 Ata una de tus piernas a una de las piernas de tu amigo.

3 Traten de caminar o saltar.

¿Qué pasó?
¿Qué aprendieron sobre colaborar?

Meet the Illustrators/Conoce a los ilustradores

Ariane Dewey has lots of rabbits visit her yard. She loves to watch them nibble dandelions. Ariane thought about those rabbits as she painted the rabbit in *The Big, Big Wall.* She says that cheery colors make her feel good. She hopes her purple rabbit and colorful animals make you happy, too.

Jose Aruego had a pet pig named Snort when he was young. "I loved that pig!" Jose says. "He was so soft and funny." When Jose had to find a way to keep Humpty Dumpty from having a big fall, he thought about Snort. He decided that a pig would be a great cushion for Humpty Dumpty!

© 1999 Todd Bigelow/Black Star

© 1999 Todd Bigelow/Black Star

Ariane Dewey tiene muchos conejos en el patio de su casa. Les encanta observarlos comerse los dientes de león. Ariana pensaba en esos conejos mientras pintaba el conejo de "No puedo bajar". Dice que los colores alegres la hacen sentir feliz. Desea que su conejo morado y los otros animales de colores también te hagan sentir feliz a ti.

Cuando José Aruego era niño tenía un cerdo llamado Snort. "¡Quería mucho a ese cerdo!", dice José. "Era suave y muy gracioso." Para encontrar un modo de ayudar a Humpty Dumpty a bajar del muro sin lastimarse, pensó en Snort. ¡Decidió que un cerdo sería un colchón perfecto para Humpty Dumpty!

About the translators
F. Isabel Campoy and Alma Flor Ada have written more than a hundred books each and each has translated many books also. But they enjoy writing and translating books in collaboration. It's great fun!

Sobre las traductoras
F. Isabel Campoy y Alma Flor Ada han escrito más de cien libros cada una, y cada una también ha traducido muchos libros. Pero les encanta cuando pueden escribir o traducir libros entre las dos. ¡Es muy divertido!

First Green Light Readers/Colección Luz Verde edition 2009

SANDPIPER and the SANDPIPER logo are trademarks of Houghton Mifflin Harcourt Publishing Company.

Green Light Readers and its logo are trademarks of Houghton Mifflin Harcourt Publishing Company, registered in the United States of America and/or other jurisdictions.

Library of Congress Cataloging-in-Publication Data is on file.
ISBN 978-0-547-25547-7
ISBN 978-0-547-25548-4 (pb)

Printed in China
SCP 10 9 8 7
4500561407

Ages 4–6
Grades: K–1
Guided Reading Level: C–D
Reading Recovery Level: 6–7

Green Light Readers
For the reader who's ready to GO!

Five Tips to Help Your Child Become a Great Reader

1. Get involved. Reading aloud to and with your child is just as important as encouraging your child to read independently.

2. Be curious. Ask questions about what your child is reading.

3. Make reading fun. Allow your child to pick books on subjects that interest her or him.

4. Words are everywhere—not just in books. Practice reading signs, packages, and cereal boxes with your child.

5. Set a good example. Make sure your child sees YOU reading.

Why Green Light Readers Is the Best Series for Your New Reader

● Created exclusively for beginning readers by some of the biggest and brightest names in children's books

● Reinforces the reading skills your child is learning in school

● Encourages children to read—and finish—books by themselves

● Offers extra enrichment through fun, age-appropriate activities unique to each story

● Incorporates characteristics of the Reading Recovery program used by educators

● Developed with Harcourt School Publishers and credentialed educational consultants

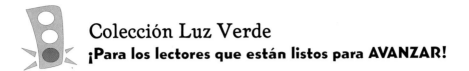

Colección Luz Verde
¡Para los lectores que están listos para AVANZAR!

Cinco sugerencias para ayudar a que su niño se vuelva un gran lector

1. Participe. Leerle en voz alta a su niño, o leer junto con él, es tan importante como animar al niño a leer por sí mismo.

2. Exprese interés. Hágale preguntas al niño sobre lo que está leyendo.

3. Haga que la lectura sea divertida. Permítale al niño elegir libros sobre temas que le interesen.

4. Hay palabras en todas partes, no sólo en los libros. Anime a su niño a practicar la lectura leyendo carteles, anuncios e información, como en las cajas de cereales.

5. Dé un buen ejemplo. Asegúrese de que su niño vea que USTED lee.

Por qué esta serie es la mejor para los lectores que comienzan

● Ha sido creada exclusivamente para los niños que empiezan a leer, por algunos de los más brillantes e importantes creadores de libros infantiles.

● Refuerza las habilidades de lectura que su niño está aprendiendo en la escuela.

● Anima a los niños a leer libros de principio a fin, por sí solos.

● Ofrece actividades de enriquecimiento, entretenidas y apropiadas para la edad del lector, creadas para cada cuento.

● Incorpora características del programa Reading Recovery usado por educadores.

● Ha sido desarrollada por la división escolar de Harcourt y por consultores educativos acreditados.

Look for more bilingual Green Light Readers!
Éstos son otros libros de la serie bilingüe Colección Luz Verde

LEVEL/NIVEL 1

Daniel's Pet/Daniel y su mascota
Alma Flor Ada/G. Brian Karas

Sometimes/Algunas veces
Keith Baker

Big Brown Bear/El gran oso pardo
David McPhail

Big Pig and Little Pig/Cerdo y Cerdito
David McPhail

What Day Is It?/¿Qué día es hoy?
Alex Moran/Daniel Moreton

LEVEL/NIVEL 2

Daniel's Mystery Egg/El misterioso huevo de Daniel
Alma Flor Ada/G. Brian Karas

Digger Pig and the Turnip/Marranita Poco Rabo y el nabo
Caron Lee Cohen/Christopher Denise

Tumbleweed Stew/Sopa de matojos
Susan Stevens Crummel/Janet Stevens

Chick That Wouldn't Hatch/El pollito que no quería salir del huev
Claire Daniel/Lisa Campbell Ernst

Get That Pest!/¡Agarren a ése!
Erin Douglas/Wong Herbert Yee

Catch Me If You Can!/¡A que no me alcanzas!
Bernard Most